CATACOMBS

CRADLE OF DARKNESS PREQUEL

ADDISON CAIN

Cover art by Dark City Designs

For the reader who is not afraid of the dark.

Catacombs is a tale of horror.

1

The whole city of New York stank.

Boulevards, vacant due to poor weather, crusted with a slush of mud and garbage. But it was the living crammed inside tightly packed houses, drinking coffee by their radios, snoring in their beds, that stung Pearl's nostrils.

She could hear them, their scratching and breaths. Worse she could smell them.

Every last one reeked under cheap perfume and lack of washing.

Patchy fur collar hitched up to cover cold ears, cloche hat doing little to keep the snow off her face, she kept her arms tight around her middle and plodded onward through the night streets. Under the threadbare coat, a fringed dress too short for common decency did nothing to keep out the winter chill. Each draft up her hem set her teeth chattering, stronger gusts earning a hiss.

Even with the smell, no matter the icy cold, she wasn't complaining.

So far, life in the big city was grand.

She'd had a busy night in the smoke-filled supper club, *Palace Delight*. Her neck may have been sore from supporting the weight of her cigarette box's strap, but she'd made two dollars. Added to the cash she'd earned the night before, and the night before that, Pearl was set to have a little extra for New Year's.

Maybe she'd get a new dress, or a nice lamp to spruce up her apartment. Better yet, some ruffled lace curtains for the room's single window—something pretty that would frame the view of the street below but keep the sun bright on her body when she slept beneath it.

She'd never had so fine a place to sleep. The walls were papered in fading floral ribbons, linoleum floors showed previous tenants' wear, but the one room abode was all hers. If she was lucky and kept to the night hours, it would be many years before neighbors even noticed she lived there. She might continue to enjoy her view of the busy street, remain sheltered, while decades crept by.

Small town life had been much more complicated. Everyone asked questions, everyone watched. Big cities, no matter how bad the inhabitants inside their borders reeked, were a boon.

If she played her cards right, no one would know that... that there was something deeply wrong with her.

All Pearl had to do was stay out of trouble.

"Hey, girly."

She'd heard him, but she knew better than to so much as raise her chin to a stranger on the street, daylight or midnight.

The Roaring Twenties offered much for a girl... but it had not changed the hardline manner of men. They were as much trouble as they'd ever been.

This one, in his pricy coat and polished wingtips, had no place wandering her working class neighborhood at 3:00 a.m. This one, huddled under the corner drug store's awning, didn't smell of bootleg whiskey; he didn't sway from too much drink. He had not come from one of the speakeasies and just gotten lost. Even from across the street, Pearl could smell that there was no lingering wash of women's perfume telling the tale of a late night dalliance with a mistress to explain his midnight stroll in foul weather.

Cocky by half, he was lurking with a purpose and by the growing beat of his heart, he'd found it: prey.

Poor women made easy targets.

Two more blocks and she'd have a locked door between herself and everyone else in Manhattan. Two more blocks and there would be nothing to worry about.

The would-be Casanova pushed from the building, cutting across the slushy street in a beeline for her. "Isn't it a little late for a stroll?"

Pearl took a sharp left, hoping he'd be wiser than to follow.

He was not.

She'd stolen a sidelong glance at his face, but did not recognize the man. It wasn't her habit to catalogue each patron she'd served. After all, they came and went night after night. Hell, she rarely spoke more than one word during her shifts unless she had to. *"Cigarette?"* A quick nod and an exchange of funds and Pearl would slip to the next table. *"Cigarette?"*

Her job wasn't to be memorable. It was to be pretty while making correct change. That's what they paid her for.

Pearl could afford her little room on the fifth floor of the Madison Building. She didn't have to make small talk or flirt. Beyond the occasional pat on the rump, patrons left her alone. No one really wanted to gab with a cigarette girl. She was part of the scenery—an ornament that made underground supper clubs like Palace Delight swanky. It was the female patrons who earned all the attention. Pearl's hair wasn't sparkling bottle blonde like theirs, it wasn't finger waved and bedecked with feathers. Hers was sleek and dark, heavy bangs across her brow, bob tight and simple.

Men didn't follow her home...

But then again, it seemed this one had been waiting for her.

"I'm talkin to you!" The stranger grabbed her elbow, yanking Pearl back so hard her heel broke on the ice. A dumpster hit her back... and everything went wrong.

Everything always went wrong.

2

Frantic, Pearl scrubbed her hands together under the tap. She couldn't get the blood off fast enough. Icy water sloshed, her hands shaking so hard little drops of pink water splattered the cracked sink, leaving a macabre mess on the porcelain.

"You've done it this time." Harshly whispered self-chastisement stuttered past chattering teeth. "You should have just let him have his fun."

Acid hit the back of her throat. One gag and her stomach emptied.

Tears running from her eyes, Pearl gripped the side of the sink. Red smeared the bowl but it was nothing to the horrid puddle of bloody vomit the drain could not draw down fast enough.

A little whirlpool grew in the mess. Running

water diluted the crimson from deep red to a light blush. All the while, hot tears ran down cold cheeks.

The man had tasted terrible.

Mottled bruises marked her cheek where the stranger had struck her. The back of her head was a pulped mush from the impact of the sidewalk. One look in the mirror told her there was more blood... in her hair, around her mouth, saturating the black wool of her only coat.

Torn throats made a mess.

Behind a split lip, a pair of delicate fangs remained distended. She'd been unable to retract them, too upset and far too scared.

Bloodshot from weeping, violet eyes stared back at her. "You have to wash off the blood. You have to wash your coat. You have to clean this room before anyone wakes up. Stop crying."

A block and a half away, a corpse was being dusted by snow, the same snow that bore a pair of uneven tracks right to her door.

At her back, the communal bathroom door was locked, but it was only a matter of time before one of the other tenants knocked so they might get ready for work. It took over an hour before water off her coat ran clear, for Pearl to wash her hair in the sink, to clean up the cuts and scrapes.

The sun was rising by the time she huddled in

her bed. Outside her only window, the storm raged on, and the world looked white and clean.

Pearl knew what was hidden under that snow, and in a matter of hours, so would the rest of New York.

BLACK AND WHITE photographs of the sprawled corpse filled front page news. He'd been found frozen solid, mild bruising on his arms and legs, throat torn open—bite marks identified on his neck. Beside the horror was the smiling image of a handsome man of quality reputation. Chadwick Parker: entrepreneur, man about town, and son of the powerful Judge Parker. He glowed with life in that photograph, handsome and chirpy—a real heartbreaker.

One conniving lie of a man.

Good Christian men didn't attack seemingly defenseless women in dark alleys. They didn't rape them.

Pearl knew better than to assume she had been the first woman he'd followed home. Over the years, how many others had he hurt?

She wasn't sorry he was dead… but she could still taste his sour blood in her mouth, could feel him shoving his cock inside her, and felt completely unclean.

Though the man who attacked her would never be able to hurt her again, she was the one left terrified.

The police were looking for the killer. For her.

The boroughs had grabbed onto the story, the press sensationalizing every known fact regarding the grotesque murder. Though the body had not been exsanguinated, it didn't matter. The official coroner's report stated that long, sharp teeth had been the weapon—that they had torn through the carotid artery while gnawing a path from left to right.

It did not resemble the bite of any known animal. The bite pattern appeared human, save two fang-like incisors.

The City Daily had been the first paper to use the word *vampire*.

Illustrious Chadwick Parker's death was treated as the most vicious murder New York had seen in ages. *Keep your children inside after dark, your womenfolk safe. Nightmares lurked in the cold dark.* No one mentioned that he'd been found with his fly open, cock out, or asked why he had been on a late night stroll through a shoddy neighborhood during a blizzard.

"Cigarette?"

Every table, every canoodling couple was whispering, boasting, making conjecture on the same thing. Her.

"Cigarette?"

Pearl had never felt physically well a time in her life, but since that man's fetid blood had pooled in her mouth, she could hardly keep anything down.

More bones than curves in her clothes, her paunchy boss was dissatisfied with what he saw. "You look like shit."

It wasn't just her flagging looks. Pearl had been jumping at shadows; she'd knocked over drinks on guests. Her time at the supper club was up, her little room with its window was going to be lost, and once again, any type of life she had tried to imagine for herself had been ruined.

She should have known better than to hope things might be different.

Pearl, her voice low so the other girls wouldn't hear, said, "Just give me one more night, sir."

"You ain't been so bad, Pearl. You show up on time, do your job... but no one wants to look at a skeleton slinging cigs."

"I'll put on more rouge, take the section farthest from the stage lights." Lightheaded, she flat out begged. "One more night, Mr. Weller. Please?"

He was unconvinced, eyeing the dark marks

under her eyes, the bony knobs of her shoulders. "You got the consumption?"

That wasn't what was wrong with her. "No, sir. I am just hungry. Winters are hard."

"Well, for Christ's sake, eat something, girl!"

She took his admonishment as approval, and flung the strap of her cigarette box over her head. Once she had it flush to her neck, she offered a close mouthed smile. "Thank you."

Rushing from the dressing rooms, she heard Mr. Weller call at her back, "The first complaint I get, you're gone, kid."

Smile glued on, everything was by the book: drop a curtsey at each table, stay moving, no lounging. Assure guests were happy. The sidelong glances, Pearl could handle, even the occasional look of disgust at her split lip. If they sneered, she smiled even bigger, fangs retracted, all her teeth on display, until they stopped sneering and looked through her.

That was how people worked; that was the world Pearl had always known.

One more night, two more dollars then she would leave her little apartment with its floral papered walls and single overhead light. In a pair of sturdy shoes, she could walk to Boston or maybe Philadelphia. It would take time, weeks, but there would be no more scary newspapers, no more feeling like the buildings were closing in around her.

She could find a job just like this one, maybe even another apartment with a window.

Or... what if she didn't leave? What if she took some time and ate a great deal? If she could fatten her cheeks up by spring, maybe Palace Delight would want her back. Without funds her room would be lost, but living on the street wasn't so bad. She'd done it before; she could do it again.

Hope, it was a vicious deceiver, but still it came to prick at her heart. It had been two weeks and no soul had knocked on her door. Perhaps New York was big enough to shield her. After all, she'd come here for a reason. The Big Apple, the Golden City she'd dreamed of for decades. Art Deco, shimmering buildings, picture shows.

Everything would be fine.

A deep breath and her smile became genuine.

True to his word, Mr. Weller fired her at the end of the shift, but not without payment. He even tucked an extra dollar in her hand out of charity. By the time she'd pulled on her coat and stepped out into the icy night, her bad turn had begun to feel manageable.

He'd hire her back, Pearl was certain. She just needed to gain some weight first. The long walk home was a good place to start. There were always rats in New York City, and they were easy enough to catch.

She snatched up two, draining each out of sight of the street. When her teeth sunk into the third, her heart stopped racing, her breath became even for the first time in days, and feeling began to come back to her frozen toes.

Starving herself out of fear of the shadows had been unwise. It was a mistake she promised herself not to repeat.

The dead, mangy creature was dropped on dirty snow. A full sigh puffed like smoke in the chilled air, Pearl leaning her head back against the brick wall of a dreary tenement. In the narrow alley, sandwiched between two tall buildings she had a small view of a pretty sky to enjoy.

"I can smell the human's blood on your coat, apostate."

Cutting off her startled shriek, a hand closed over her mouth... a hand attached to an arm that had grown from the wall at her back.

Screaming behind the clamp of rough fingers, Pearl threw a terrified glance side to side in a desperate attempt to see who'd caught her.

Nobody was there, only a wall and a garbage bin.

Fear elongated fangs behind her lips, kohled

lashes spiked with cake mascara went so wide, the whites of her eyes shone bright in the dark.

The feeling of jagged mortar grinding against her spine melted away, morphing from ice cold brick to the firm body of a man.

He hoisted her upward, despite her frantically kicking legs, while silent figures materialized to her left and her right.

Brick met her face, cheek split, teeth cracked.

Dazed from the blow, Pearl's mouth gaped and her eyes settled on an angel.

The being, the stranger, gripped her chin, his fingers distorting her cheeks as he smiled. That grin promised pain, the torments of hell, and was the most terrifying thing Pearl had seen in her long, laborious life.

Begging was not beneath her. "I never meant to hurt anyone."

From the monster's mouth, a milky white pair of razor sharp teeth grew long and menacing.

Two long fangs just like hers.

It could not be…

It couldn't.

Things like her did not exist. She was sick, that was all. She was sick and needed the absolution of God to save her from her deformity and perverse hungers.

Instinct would disagree with her. One look at

those fangs and Pearl hissed, began to fight in earnest, and was punished horribly.

The smiling man jammed his fingers into her mouth. Gagging when he hooked her fang, she tried to bite. It took several hard jerks, but with a final twisting wrench, he ripped her tooth straight from her skull.

Gums torn, the socket open and spurting blood, Pearl wailed.

No pain she'd ever known compared to this.

Her second fang was gouged out, her cheek ripped fully apart from corner to ear when the man laughing in her face caught his sharpened nail on the flesh.

The angel had no interest in her words, the question in her eyes, or her gurgled prayers... only her agony.

3

Feet dragging over pavement, a stream of blood poured from her mouth to mark the path. In the time it took to bring her to this place, she had counted them. Three men with angelic faces and evil hearts had hauled her the distance, and not a single soul had seen.

Dangling between them, the best she could do was press a hand to her maimed face, swallow the constant flow of blood collecting in her mouth, and weep. Her attacker had taken more than her fangs, he had taken her misguided hope that there might be answers to her life—that there might be more for her than year upon year of isolation and loneliness.

There were others like her.

How could she have never known?

Even as they'd beat her, Pearl had tried to ask

them what they were. But these men, these glowing angels, were so much stronger and possessed no pity for what they'd deemed *an apostate*.

She was going to die, be ravaged. If what he'd done to her face was any example, it would be a painful and brutal end.

Sticky crimson ran down her chin, over her neck, staining her clothes. Trying to keep her jaw together despite torn tendons and shredded skin, she failed at speech. Useless lolling tongue only smeared gore from ear to ear, mixed it with her tears.

Tearing the fabric, her coat was yanked down skinny arms, the girl left in only the supper club's flashy uniform and torn stockings. And that was how they made her walk down the dark, littered alley where she expected they would murder her and leave her to rot.

It was not a good place to die.

Hair in the grip of the one who'd torn out her teeth, head bent back, she saw one last view of the stars.

The man began to chant.

Groaning in protest of the unnatural bend of her spine engorged a bubble of blood on her cheek. It popped, her bones cracked in symphony with her captor's guttural pronunciations, and the world lurched.

Vision distorted, walls leaning toward her as if ready to crumble and crush her to dust, Pearl watched the awful world twist in upon her and turn her inside out.

This must be death.

A moment later, it was over.

The grim reaper had not come. Her heart still banged against her chest, her blood still poured from her ruined mouth, and pain only grew.

They were no longer standing in the snow, hidden between tight row houses. Now, uneven, time-worn masonry was under her feet, her scream echoing off an arched stone roof, with not a speck of sky to be seen.

The cry died, and all around them the sound of softly traded conversation, the noise of footfalls echoing as if they stood in a great cathedral replaced it.

A church?

But there were no crosses or priests, only a congregation of strangers watching as she was dragged deeper into the sanctum.

Maybe she had died and this was how she was to be judged, bleeding and broken before heaven's shining hosts.

As she was dragged forward, she caught a glimpse of the quiet crowd watching her advance. She found the gazes of curious strangers.

She disgusted them. Some even sniffed her way, sneering.

A sharp kick hit the back of her legs; knees knocked into stone so hard her teeth snapped and the pain in her jaw doubled. Hunched over, Pearl clutched her torn cheek, pathetic, scared, and completely confused.

The angel who'd torn out her teeth and ripped open her face shouted so all might hear, "This apostate is responsible for abandoning the remains of Chadwick Parker where humans would find them. I have brought it before you, my lord, as you ordered." He threw her stolen coat on the ground before them. "And here is the proof. The dead human's blood is matted into her coat."

Tightening his fingers until her scalp burned, the man jerked her head back so all might look upon her ruined face.

The men and women gathered around whispered excitedly, but Pearl saw none of it, heard nothing. From the moment her head had been flung back, her eyes were fixed in horror, glued to the *thing* that waited at the head of the room.

This was not heaven and she was not to be judged by God...

It was dim, the chamber lit only with gas lamps instead of the popular electric bulb, but she saw the visage of the fallen one. Light flickered, drawing the pits and edges of its face into stark relief. More hideous than any imagined devil, it spoke, glowing red eyes engaged upon the man who held her down. "Ten days it took you to find the one responsible, and all you have to show me is one unremarkable, toothless female."

Towering over her, her captor answered his liege. "Weak as it is, it obviously has not fed in days. My lord, it thought to hide from your authority. Once it emerged, the apostate was captured easily, defanged with minimal effort. Its teeth I offer to you."

Like the shabby coat, the bloodied pair of elongated incisors were tossed to bounce like dice toward the feet of the monstrosity.

The *gift* was ignored.

The devil turned his eyes to her instead. The power of that burning red gaze traveled like a living thing to settle on her bloodied face.

It stared through her, unmoving where it rotted in its seat. Rope-like muscle encased prominent bones—as if the creature's flesh had wilted in the grave. Grotesque as it was, its form remained massive.

It wanted to see the whole of her face, demanded that she lower her hand—Pearl could hear him whispering into her mind, urging absolute obedience. There was no possible question of resisting. Weak, her fingers slipped from where she'd relentlessly tried to hold her jaw together, the damage on display for all to see.

Her captor had called her toothless; Pearl grasped the slander was meant to shame. It did. She was almost as hideous as the demon.

Incapable of forming words, incapable of screaming, she could not move, not a muscle, when an arm stretched impossibly far across the room. Boney fingers slid over the ruined side of her face. He probed, snagging her bloody lip to prod the empty sockets and the bits of exposed bone between torn gums.

Her throbbing, horrible pain faded into nothing.

An unexpected caress of the devil's thumb wiped away her steady trail of tears, the long yellowed nail at the end careful not to scratch.

Just as the pain had vanished, her fear began to drain away until she was empty of all things.

Red, scorching eyes were all she might fathom, her end and her beginning. Nothing else mattered; nothing existed but that rotting devil and her.

A flicker of satisfaction and his interrogation began. "Child?"

The mummified monstrosity cupped her jaw, holding it in place to facilitate her speech. Tongue thick, Pearl found herself answering without hesitation. "Yes?"

Raspy and horrid, his voice slithered through her ears. "Did you slay the human, Chadwick Parker, and leave his body on the street?"

She blinked once. More tears fell from red-rimmed eyes, her voice vacant. "He was hurting me. It was the only way to make him stop."

The unblinking monster projected his pleasure, looking upon her as if beholding something truly worth devouring. "Tell me what happened."

Still as stone, legs awkward under her, Pearl found herself leaning into the corpse-like touch. "It was dark. I didn't want to talk to him."

"And?"

"He forced me down, tore up my skirt so fast he was inside me before I could scream." No one would have come even had they heard her cry for help. People didn't go down dark alleys in search of damsels in distress.

Humans ignored screams in the night.

The demon answered her unspoken thoughts. "Because they are nothing but animals."

"It hurt."

There was no change in the fierce expression of the creature who commanded the room, only more demands. "Why leave the body?"

What had the devil expected her to do with it? "I had to crawl away before anyone saw."

"And in doing so broke a crucial law." If

such a thing were possible, he seemed even more immense, her immediate world nothing but withered lips and glowing eyes full of fire. "Like any vassal under my rule, you must be punished."

Her words came jumbled, as if from a drunken mouth. "I'm scared."

The beast almost seemed to smile. "An apostate should be scared. You'll be lucky to survive what's coming."

"I don't understand." Pearl blinked, a twin trail of tears escaping dazed eyes.

"You entered my city without permission, hid from my authority, and thought to hunt here, leaving a mess humans identified correctly. Is that clear enough for you?"

No. Even with her mind filled by the will of something powerful, Pearl disputed what the monstrosity had said. "Vampires are not real. I'm deformed. I'm sick. If I am faithful, God will have mercy on me."

The monster chuckled, then seemed to catch something in her thoughts that stopped his mirth. "You believe such ridiculousness to be true."

Sniffing, feeling her mind mush as the monster dug deeper, Pearl wept. "I want to go home."

Utter silence grew between them. Glowing eyes burned, the creature's concentration palpable. It clawed its way through her head, scraping through memory, picking apart what she was.

It startled.

At length, words came from the demon's mouth. "You have brought me a daywalker. It doesn't know what it is."

A ripple moved around her, strange enough to fractionally distract the girl kneeling on the flagstones. Incessant buzzing murmurs grew, *daywalker* whispered again and again.

"This one is to serve her sentence in solitary confinement." An announcement came from the throne, the room silenced by their rotting lord. "See that she is fed, Malcolm, and seal the door. Brick it shut."

The dreamlike quality that had invaded Pearl's senses came to an abrupt end. When the gnarled hand of the monster receded, her pain roared back to life. Scooped into the crushing arms of the stone-faced angel who offered no pity, she was carried away from the mob and deep into the dark underground.

4

A nchored to the floor by spilt wax, the flicker of a single candle offered the damp crypt's solitary illumination.

Pressed against the opposite wall, another sorry soul shared Pearl's gloom—a man, cowering and crying, whom Malcolm had shoved into the cell shortly before he'd locked her away. Together, they both listened to the splat and bang of brick piled up on the other side of the room's only exit.

Their eyes met over that candle, both aware this was their end.

A moldering cot under her, Pearl rocked, arms tight around her knees, as if the pain of her cheek and gums might be soothed by such movement.

Nothing helped.

She was in agony.

"Please... don't hurt me." Like a cornered animal, the man—and unlike the other things she'd seen upstairs, he was a man—stared at her with wide, bloodshot eyes.

He was petrified.

Pearl could hear his heart, the thrum of his blood loud, but she paid him no mind, too wrapped up in her own misery to care.

The panicked stranger watched, bracing, as if she were going to leap up to devour him. "It wasn't my fault... I told them it wasn't my fault. I don't want to die."

Head throbbing, she snapped, words lisped by slack, swollen lips, "No one wants to die. It doesn't change the fact that everyone does."

He sputtered out a list of excuses as if she might exonerate him of whatever crime landed him in the same room as her. "The boy. Yes, I took him... but I didn't mean to kill him. I don't belong here, dame. You gotta believe me. I do not deserve this!"

Pearl wanted silence. "The *thing* upstairs would disagree."

The fretting human was so much larger than her, but he cowered as if a slurring, toothless girl was the greatest threat in existence. "Please don't eat me. I want to go home..."

"Eat you?" She scoffed. The taste of men was foul and this one smelled especially vile. "I am not going to eat you. Find your way out. Go home for all I care."

He took her word to heart, and like a fool, tried to pry open the door. "It won't budge."

Nor would it.

It was bricked shut.

Unless he was set free in a few days, the male would die from lack of water and food. Then she would have his corpse for company and the sweet smelling rot that putrefied the dead. And it would grow quiet—fitting that they'd shoved her into an old tomb.

Pearl had to admit, the candle was an interesting touch... one last moment of light soon to snuff out. The stone walls held no windows, only the notched shelves of a coffin-less crypt, the cot, and the dirt.

When she'd first been dragged into this horrible place, before her interview with the devil, the stone structure looked like a church. Now she was certain it had been before being desecrated. It was the feel to the place: ungodliness, desperation. Bad things had happened in these halls over various, sundry years. How many other old tombs held prisoners bricked away to rot? How many of them had one final candle?

Pearl considered burning her clothing to extend the light, but it seemed pointless. Dark would intercede soon enough, and she'd rather be warm—as warm as one can be in a freezing box—than hold onto false hope.

Knees under her chin, she watched the flame spark on the last fragment of wick, until it was only an ember. The tang of smoke in the air, the space grew stygian. Eyes open or closed, it made no difference. There was nothing to see.

But there was something to fear.

Now that all the light had been snuffed out, she could feel *it* watching from the dark.

Before having her cast down into this pit, *it* had looked at her, the feel of *its* cold hands had caressed her face. She could see the glowing red eyes, the devil peering at her from the lightless abyss. And then he was there, growing from the shadows, seeping up from the floor as if pulling darkness into the form of his desire.

Screwing her eyes shut, Pearl buried her face against her knees.

Standing over her, towering and projecting agitation, the demon hissed, "You were ordered to be fed. Why is this human still living?"

The human started screaming.

Pearl shrieked herself when a cold touch landed on her stinging scalp. "I can't!"

The caress of talon tipped fingers tripped over her skull. The feel of wind moved through her hair, the creature's nails teasing a lock of blood-matted sable. "Have you not learned how to bleed them without using your teeth? It is not difficult to open a vein."

Why was it touching her, lightly following the shell of her ear with a claw?

Petrified, Pearl tried not to breathe, not to move. Still the red-eyed monster explored, dipping his yellowed fingernail lower to explore the curve of her throat before pulling away.

Moments later, across the room there was a wet, squelched squeal from the human.

His screaming stopped.

"There, I have done it. His throat is open. Drink."

Pearl refused to budge.

Another threat was issued. "Do you wish me to force you, child? Obey me at once."

Her disgust was obvious.

"So be it." The *thing* took her by the hair, tilting her head back. Something hot and wet dripped on her cheeks. Papery lips fell on hers, the devil's mouth opening so coppery fluid might pour from him to her.

Gagging, Pearl tried to push him off. It was no use. He was going to drown her if she didn't swallow. Obeying, blood went down her throat like acid all the way to her belly. The instant the demon pulled away, she retched, every last drop spit up on her lap.

"I see..."

It drew away, Pearl curling into a sobbing ball on the cot.

She didn't need to see him to know what the red-eyed monster was doing. Sounds of slurping, of human pain, mixed together until the dying man's stuttering heartbeat told the story.

When it was done, a corpse thudded against the floor, and once again *it* slithered closer. "Shall I offer a female? Can you drink from them?"

In sharp jerks, Pearl shook her head.

A smile altered the monster's growl. "What of children, babies... do they not tempt you?"

She was going to throw up again. "God, help me."

Again he dared to lay his hand atop her head, to finger the spot where chunks of hair had been ripped out by his minion. A laugh layered the devil's offer. "And what of me, do I entice your attention?"

Pearl vehemently refused, shrinking from the feel of unyielding arms slowly encircling her shoulders. The cot creaked, the weight of the demon settling close enough those glowing red eyes hovered inches from her face.

When instinct moved her to struggle, to kick and scream as if she stood even a chance of forcing the vile thing from her, the devil seeped into her mind. He manipulated her just as he'd done when she'd been dumped before his throne—slipping behind her barrier of fear—taking it away until his prey lay still and calm.

He had her quiet. He had her controlled. "Tell me your name in this life."

Torn lips parted. "...Pearl."

"And you find me so repulsive, Pearl?" The creature did not require a reply. Instead he offered a lesson. "I offered you dark, so you might not gaze upon what you openly recoiled from at first sight, and still you cower. I offered you food, the comfort of my presence, a gentle touch... yet still you dare to refuse my attention"—the red-eyed demon let that horrid gaze go to her ruined mouth—"my Pearl."

Powerless, she unfolded when his body shifted against her, bowing back at the feel of a light grip about her throat. Unable to see beyond the glow of his eyes, she could only feel—the chill of him, the whisper of his breath on her face.

Pinned to the mattress, Pearl lay listless while his fingers both crept and cradled. He moved her at will, laying her head to the crook of his shoulder, her legs entangled in the tattered fabric of his rotting garments.

"So lovely..." He was more enraptured than she,

fingertips ghosting over the arch of her brow, teasing the fringe of her lashes.

The icy touch receded, but not before the tatters of her jaw were made to part.

There was a crunch, a sound similar to the snaps of splitting wood, and the thing began to bleed. Having rent its own tongue straight down the middle, it laved it against the roof of Pearl's mouth, over her teeth, until the sweetest flavor she had ever tasted began to trickle down her throat.

Blackberry cordial. Melted ice cream. It was like sipping moonlight laced with wine.

Sluggishly, thick blood flowed, the forked tongue of her tormentor toying with hers. She found herself keening, pants of trapped air puffing from her nostrils as she succumbed to hunger and drank. Sucking his tongue, frustrated when the source of nourishment healed before she'd had her fill, she tried to bite.

Her teeth could not keep his flesh open no matter how she gnawed.

Without her fangs, she could do little more than inspire a rumbling chuckle in the demon's chest.

His invasion of her mind withdrew, the hunger remained. Pearl found it was she who clung to him, she who lapped at his mouth, greedy for more.

That was his trick...

He stole his arms back, left her lying dazed and

starving on the cot. "Are you not going to kiss me, Pearl?"

She'd swallowed enough to feel the effects of a sip of darkness. The skin of her cheeks was pulling together, itching as it mended... but her belly was still so hollow.

It wasn't enough.

Daring to admit confusion, repulsion, and delight, Pearl grew drunk. "I'm still hungry."

A sharp nail gently grazing back and forth over her collarbones, the creature smiled. It leaned down, mouth working over her throat, teasing gently at her pulse point. "Shall I slit my throat so you can feed?"

The instant desire for a deeper drink was at odds with clearer thought. What he offered was not what it seemed.

Breathless, eyes open and unblinking in the dark, she felt a sharp nail graze over her nipple and complete revulsion returned. The demon's hand crept lower as if to delve between her legs.

Insidious fear bloomed right back to life, licking through her, ruining any chance Pearl might have had at further reason. She did not beg for mercy, or scream when a talon pierced through her undergarment. She was past that point when a separate flash of claw raked through leathery skin.

The monster sliced himself so deeply, a river spurt over her face.

Perhaps if she had not been so hungry, Pearl might have exercised self-control, but one tiny taste, his offering dripping over her lips, and she latched on despite the dry digit wriggling deeper into her body.

Fixed to his wound, she opened the fissure of flesh, jabbing her tongue into the meat of his neck to force the fountain wider. Greedily she gorged, never having known a meal that fulfilled and warmed as this deep drink did.

While she gorged, it pawed at her clothing, picking it apart with nail and fist until breasts popped free of her dress and cold air moved over bruised thighs. He stripped her naked, the scraps of her clothing left to bunch under their bodies, and then he did the same to his own ancient garments.

She would have drunk him dry, utterly unaware of his actions had his palm not settled like sandpaper over her breast. One scrape of his dry-skinned touch grating her nipple and she whimpered, lips parting from his neck.

It felt... odd.

The pebbled tip of her breast tingled, responded to a pinching roll of the monster's forefinger and thumb. When his thighs purposefully maneuvered to her parted legs, when pressure was placed against her mound, Pearl found she had no focus to resist.

Not with that delicious fountain oozing to fill up her mouth.

While she fed, the monster spoke. The things he said, had Pearl been beyond bloodlust, would have set her screaming. "I have waited an eternity for you, *kara sevde*. Your blood will be my blood, your cunt dripping nightly from my attention. Every last part of you will be saturated in me, in your lord. Forget your God, and worship at my feet."

When her belly grew full and her mouth fell from his throat, Pearl was given no absolution.

It was a devious seduction; the red-eyed one having waited so it might look upon her face when his cock speared straight into her unsuspecting body.

The shock was less from pain and more from astonishment. Pearl's mouth fell open, head thrown back at the intrusion. The deceitful monstrosity had taken raw advantage, leaving her cramped around the dead meat inside her.

Her female parts... the slit he'd called her cunt... felt stretched unmercifully. The burning wash of sensation didn't ease no matter how hard she tried to crawl out from under the unwavering glowing red eyes.

There was no negotiation. He did not try to soothe. Instead the creature roughly jerked his hips, ground against her, and restrained with ease. When his thrust grew more than experimental, when her breasts bounced and friction built, *it* began to groan.

The hissing breaths and pleasure saturated hums were grotesque, the way her body responded sickening.

She was engorged, nerves tingling, tightening, fear and hunger feeding the buildup. If the ruthless pounding did not stop, Pearl was going to split in two.

Tears leaked from her eyes when the ripple of muscle where he invaded began to seize. Unsure what was happening, she called out to her God.

The devil laughed.

Pain crept through nerves, coming to life in her gut, and forming into something obscene.

She wasn't screaming in agony at all, it was something else—something foreign.

Pulling out until only the tip of his instrument was tucked in her sopping slit. Once she'd found her breath, staring up in horror, it began all over again.

Every time she was on the cusp of abandon, the devil took away what tore her apart. It may have been hours, it may have been days, before Pearl understood his brand of torment.

It was never going to end until she begged for the very thing she found so disgusting.

Sobbing, she asked for mercy. He told her what to say—filthy words worse than any she'd picked up from men in the supper club fell from swollen lips, desperation lacing every last entreaty until the monster reared and redoubled his effort. The instant she discovered her first climax, he put his teeth to her neck, puncturing soft skin.

His cock kicked and he gushed.

He didn't drink much, but exhaustion unlike she'd ever known made Pearl's eyes heavy and her limbs useless. The dusty groan of a beast still filled the air, and it was not until he'd fully savored his pleasure, that the demon laid his lips to the very skin he'd bruised.

Small kisses peppered flesh tender from the scrape of his chest. Gently, he sucked her nipple, tongue teasing, teeth nipping. Warm breath fanned over her flesh as he sighed. "How I wish you would remember the glory of this moment as I will, but alas, that cannot be."

While she lay struck and horrified, it rolled its hips to tease out a cruel reminder that she had enjoyed his blood, his cock, and even his brutality.

The room was once again cold, Pearl aware of the hideous thing that had fucked her raw and the threat his last words posed. "I don't want to die."

If pure evil might be sweet, the demon made an attempt, cooing at her gently. "You are too valuable to break. No, my Pearl, you will be mine forever."

5

W aking groggy, Pearl turned in her bed and snuggled deeper into soft blankets for warmth. A dull ache irritated her gums, and absently she tongued the spot, only to find two teeth were missing. Not just any teeth, but the sharp teeth she'd tried herself many times in life to wrench out.

The thing that made people afraid of her when she got scared or angry...

Her fangs, were gone.

Throwing back the covers, her hand flew to her mouth, and the shock over the nagging discomfort was replaced with absolute bewilderment.

She had no idea where she was.

There was light, golden and soft around the strangest room she'd ever seen. Not a single window contributed to the glow, only weighty gilded candelabras, ancient in design, strewn about. A small portion of the candles had burned to stubs, beside them fresh tapers with wicks white and untouched waited to be lit.

She was in a bed larger than any she'd ever seen. It gave off the subtle fragrance of teakwood and was foreign in its design and height. Above it draped a canopy, heavy curtains of embroidered gold, tied and gathered by anchors implanted in crumbling stone walls. Layered around her body were red velvet coverlets, the pillows sumptuous and plentiful at her back.

Between the candelabras and bed, there was scant other furniture in the small room. A writing desk took center stage, a thick tome open atop it. Beside the blotter were pens, a brush, a hand mirror. Even a pot of rouge.

There was more, other things littering hoary, somber stone. Strange *fabric* against her skin...

Over her breasts was not the familiar uniform the Palace Delight had charged her three dollars for, but black chiffon. So sheer her nipples were on display, it hung gathered at her shoulders like some tart's version of a nightgown.

Someone had dressed her in this. Someone had put her in this room.

Memories of a man holding her down in the

snow, of pain, left her colder than ice. Had he brought her here after he'd finished? Hadn't she killed him?

There had been so much blood…

A sour flavor.

What was going on?

There was no exit save a wooden door straight from a medieval movie set. Leaning against the portal, half concealing the frame, was a massive mirror. Like the candelabras, it was overly ornate, gaudy, and looked far too heavy for her to move.

Untangling from the covers, Pearl's feet landed on a woven rug of burgundy and cobalt. Under the brightly colored wool lay rushes that crunched the instant she placed weight on her foot. With her every step, the drying grass's scent mingled with the room's must, the smoke from the candles, and the smell of ambergris.

Her wrists had been perfumed.

Nose to her arm, she inhaled, and noticed an ornate ring sparkling on her hand. She had not felt the glimmering collection of stones, but now it held her complete attention. The piece was much larger than the art deco jewelry in fashion; the stones were much grander. In the center was a ruby rounded smooth, as big as an eye, anchored by tarnished gold and surrounded by seed pearls.

Unlike the other objects in the room, something

about it was *wrong*. It pinched and felt unwelcome. Yanking the ring from her finger, she cast it off as if it were cursed.

Chest rising and falling in panicked breaths, Pearl tried to make sense of it all—of the stone walls half hidden by pastoral paintings, of the feeling of foreboding—and knew this was a bad place.

Hurtling toward the low, arched exit, she found herself caught by the mirror before her shaking hand might even try the knob.

There was a reason the colossal furnishing had been left there... the door was only an enticement. The true aim of the object was to get her close enough to the reflective glass to see.

Her hair was no longer clipped into a sleek bob. Wrongly, it hung past her shoulders, tangled from sleep. The shape of her body was foreign as well. Where were her prominent ribs, the dark marks under her eyes?

Yes, she'd always been attractive in her way, but she had never glowed with health. She'd never had soft curves or full breasts.

Blue eyes lacked the makeup she'd painstakingly applied every day. She didn't need the kohl, or the cake mascara. Had she shown up to the Palace Delight looking like *this*, Mr. Weller would have never fired her. He would have promoted her.

Hell, he would have married her.

"Most nights when I come to you, you have yet to look in the mirror. It's the journal that habitually grabs your attention, Pearl."

An unladylike shriek came from the girl, Pearl spinning to find a stranger stepping toward her.

Pinched between long fingernails, he held the ring she'd rejected. He offered it to her, smiling and splendid, but all she could see were his eyes.

They were red as fire and so utterly wrong she thought she might be sick.

Putting the desk between them, she took in the face of what every last woman in Manhattan would deem perfection. He was beautiful, cheeks shaven smooth, dark hair slicked back in the style of Gary Cooper—more handsome than Gary Cooper, if such a thing were possible. But he was not dressed as a gentleman. In nothing more than a long black robe tied with a sash at his waist, he was hardly dressed at all.

Something about him, beyond the blood red of his eyes, set the hairs on the back of her neck to attention.

His gaze lost the crimson glow, growing into an almost soft brown as he smiled. "I am Darius."

Red eyes, cold stone, and the scream of a dying man in the pitch black... fragments of memory echoed until the room with its finery looked like something else.

A tomb full of monsters.

"Where am I?"

His gaze tripped over her breasts, admiration all over his face. "I did not mean to startle you, Pearl. Come closer so I might see that you are well."

Dizzy, Pearl put her fingers to her cheek. It had been torn open last she recalled, held together by a red-eyed demon who'd crept through her mind and asked her his questions.

A single candle in a room colder than death.

A corpse's body moving against and inside her.

Mumbling to herself, caught between the present and the past, Pearl said, "The light went out and you came in."

And now golden light was abundant, the red-eyed demon was back, wrapped up in beautiful skin and walking toward her with a smile.

She dared to counter his advance with a retreat, and a face that was beautiful grew twisted with impatience. "Kneel, my Pearl."

It was as if some unseen force shoved her down. Legs hit the floor, the girl folding downward, her body utterly out of her control at his command.

"Look at me."

In the attitude of prayer, body prostrate and hands clasped before her, Pearl stared up at what had come to tower over her. A manicured hand reached forward as if to bless her.

His fingers were warm, soft, but a ghostly touch of memory came with it. Sandpaper, claws... pain in the dark.

And then memory of something that wasn't pain. The intimate sensation twinging in her belly was profane, as was the urge to reach between her thighs and rub.

The man chuckled. "Your mind goes interesting places, dear girl. You are afraid and aroused all at once. It makes you taste particularly delicious. Are you trying to tempt me? I would hate to neglect my treasure."

A pulsing heart grew between her legs, sweat breaking out over her brow as Pearl's breath grew shallow. "Is this hell?"

The stranger raised her from the floor. "If it was, would it be your hell or mine?"

With no preamble, he cupped her breast, his tongue wetting his lower lip.

Impulse brought her to raise her arm. She struck him.

All her strength, and the slap didn't so much as turn his chin. Instead, it inspired ravenously heated eyes and a growing smile full of unsavory promises

Run.

But there was nowhere to go.

The door met her back, the man pressed indecently to her front. Lips came to her ear, warm breath offering, "You may lie upon the bed, legs obediently parted, and I'll see that you feel the pleasure of my mouth where you itch. Or, you may kiss my hand and beg my forgiveness for such rudeness, and I might find it in my heart to be patient and see to your other needs first." His hand came to her face, taking her jaw with enough strength to be more sinister than sweet. "But never strike me, child, unless you'd like your night to be one of suffering."

She had known enough pain in her life. Seeking mercy from a thing that terrified her very soul, she beseeched, "Please. I didn't mean to kill that man."

Smirking menacingly, the stranger, Darius, captured her fingers. "Darling, kara sevde." He did not break eye contact. The ring she'd thrown slid home, nestled where he desired it to be, and then he lifted her fingertips and kissed them. "You have a weakness for desiring to live in the past. I require you live only in this moment. What came before and what will come after do not matter. They do not exist to you. Nothing but this room and my attention exist to you."

"I don't understand."

His hand came back to her breast, the red-eyed man daring her to slap him again. "What is there to understand? I am your everything, and you are my beloved treasure."

Skin crawling, she knew more than anything that she wanted out of that room—just as much as she wanted the man to stop kneading her breast. "I don't want to be your treasure."

A low growl, demonic in nature preceded, "Where is your gratitude today, Pearl? I do not appreciate when you wake in a temper."

"I belong to God."

"And what would God do for my darling one? Where are you safer than here? Where could you be more comfortable? As you are, you're buried so far under the city no soul could ever find you. No one will take you from me. No others will know the taste of sunshine in your veins. I made them all forget. You exist in my world alone."

Eyes cast to the ceiling, she offered a prayer. "Jesus, help me."

"There is no God for you but me. There is no heaven waiting for you. I own your soul and your body. I own your mind, daywalker... your blood." All of this was spoken gently, lovingly, each word acidic and tainted by evil. His voice burned her. "I am your life and your only reason for existence. Without my care, you would live alone in this tomb for eternity... forgotten by the thing you would pray to."

Stroking her hair, ignoring her incantations to the Christian Lord, he cooed, "Your affection will earn a reward. Give me a kiss and cease these theatrics at once. I'm giving you one chance to avoid punishment today."

She shook her head.

He caught her hair with clawed fingers and forced her neck to bend where he willed it. On the straining column of her throat he licked a path all the way to her ear. "I told you to kiss me, Pearl."

Breath shaking, unable to move from the strength of his grip in her hair, Pearl whimpered, stopped the prayer, and gasped when a little sting set her neck to jumping.

"Delicious. Your fear is almost worth the trouble." A tongue ran over her pulsing vein. "But I have another flavor in mind today."

Stepping back, he released her hair, smirking as she sagged against rough stone.

Twisted in his sweet offer was a much more sinister threat. "Last chance. Kiss me, beg my forgiveness for your rudeness, and let's begin anew."

Pearl didn't want pain, she'd known enough in her life. She didn't want terror, but it was staring her in the face. Swallowing, certain she was going to be ill, she reached for the door handle at her back, and found it frozen.

It would not be moved.

If he was keen to the scrambling of her fingers at her back he said nothing, the gloriously beautiful devil seemingly patient.

Brick it shut, he'd said. She remembered the sounds, the human trying to claw his way out. She remembered what this room truly was.

A crypt to be buried in.

There was no way out.

God did not hear her prayers.

Her tongue tripped, and out of her mouth came the only slice of salvation she could reach. "I'm sorry for my rudeness."

"And?"

He may have been handsome, but she remembered the monster who'd spoken to her from the throne. It was almost impossible to lean forward and press a kiss to the man's cheek, certain he would stink like a rotting corpse.

Instead, he smelled of sandalwood and fresh blood.

Something about it made her mouth water and brought a tingle to empty tooth sockets. The prickling became a sharp pinch, two small teeth descending to burst through the gum-line and end as useless points too short to be of any use.

Chuckling, the demon drove her back until her head hit the impenetrable door and his tongue was deep in her mouth. He licked each smear of blood, toying with her stumped fangs as if she'd performed some cute act.

It was less a kiss and more a scouring, the whole time red glowing eyes staring straight into hers.

With one final tongue curled lick, he pulled away, teasing, "Hungry, are you?"

Yes? No. She wasn't ravenous, not in the ways she remembered. But under the terror, she was hungry for *something*—something sweet and filling that healed the soul and fattened the flesh.

Something that made it all better.

She wanted that delicious succor as one would pine for a drug. Breaking eye contact, she looked to the stranger's neck, whining low in her throat and completely lost in unfamiliar need.

Stretching forward, Pearl caught herself inches from setting her useless teeth to the devil's flesh when it gave a warning tut.

He took her chin, tapping her nose as he counseled. "It is a good thing you stopped yourself this time. Never take what isn't offered. Though I never allow your mind to cling to the memory, I promise you, it is the worst of punishments I can offer."

Again her blood went cold. "You make it sound as if I have been here a long time."

Rolling words full of smoke and brimstone, he asked, "What did I tell you about time? The only time of any worth in your life are the moments you spend with me."

"How many moments have there been?"

"Not nearly enough."

What had he done to her in the days she'd lost in this place? What would he do? "And you punish me?"

"When I feel so inclined. But I'm not eager to harm your sweet body tonight." Turning his back and walking across the room to settle his mass on the edge of the overly large, ornate bed, he said, "This evening I have come to my pet for pleasure. If you please me, I will let you drink your fill. Disappoint my appetites, and I will bring you great pain. For I have no patience for an insolent treasure. Save yourself the torment." He crooked a finger, calling her forward. "Come here."

She knew nothing about pleasing men. The men who had used her, had done only that—leaving her sullied and shamed as they'd tucked their cocks away and abandoned her where she'd bled.

It was to be one pain or another.

Pearl could submit now and spare the girl who would wake tomorrow to some unforeseen horror. Or she could refuse, earn the demon's wrath and know suffering immediately.

She *was* in hell.

Killing Chadwick Parker had landed her here.

One foot in front of the other, ten steps total, and she stood before her tormenter.

Darius took her wrist, brought it to his lips to gently kiss, before yanking her face first into the mattress. Tense and trembling she lay as she fell, cheek to red velvet. He stood and moved behind her, flipping the girl face up.

"It's like the first time every time, isn't it? My Pearl is practically a virgin. Always fresh. Always frightened." Creeping over her body, he took her gauze-draped nipple into his mouth for a sharp suck. Once it popped free, he teased, "But I know how to make the virgin a whore."

Eyes to the bed curtains, fingers fisted in the sleeves of the man's robe, Pearl tried to lay still. Let him do what he may, let him take, knowing the night would end and she would forget all of it.

Tomorrow would be better.

6

There was no tomorrow.

The first time he'd fucked her had been slow, deviously tender. It didn't feel like the same frightening creature who'd taunted, threatened, and mocked.

He took her as one takes a lover, a cherished wife. Long kisses, sweet touches, even the sweeping entry of his engorged cock had been smooth. Long nailed fingers drifted over her body, delving into places that brought unimaginable pleasures. She could have wept knowing love like that might truly exist in the world and that she'd never know it.

This *thing* didn't love her. The proof was there in his violence when he'd grown bored of soft moans and fluttering cunts.

With his semen dripping from her slit, Pearl had

panted, satisfied in body from a kind of release she'd never known.

Or had known many times but could not remember.

He'd pulled out, kissed her on the mouth as if she'd behaved perfectly, then abruptly shunted his arm straight inside the place he'd just used—all of his fingers, his fist to the wrist as she bucked, screaming for him to get them out.

Ripped and bleeding, he'd just as brusquely tore them away, leaving her hole gaping, oozing a blend of her pulped flesh, his cum, and a steady flow of blood.

Her womb had been torn, her tunnel ruined, and with his teeth growing long and sinister, he met the screaming girl's eye and watched her try to escape. He licked up the mess, swallowed bits of flesh, and savored her every cry.

Healing under those teeth and tongue, her insides knit back in place, her vaginal passage grew once again tight, and all the damage his nails had done disappeared into new flesh that was pink and engorged from vigorous attention.

The cruel lover concentrated his tongue near the top of her sex. What he did there arched her back in both loathing and unbearable sensation.

Restraining her with ease, he licked and sucked her swollen nub, twisting her nerves until she came, sobbing for mercy.

He stared down at the quivering mouth of her cunt, smirking at the pink fluttering lips that framed a hole empty and aching no matter how hard she'd climaxed. Shelving his chin atop her mound, Darius ran his gaze upward over her wildly heaving ribs to meet frantic eyes. "You wet the bed."

Too far gone in her terror, all she could do was sob and wildly shake her head. She even begged him for help as if he were not the root of all her torment.

"Poor dear." His weight came off of her thighs, Pearl curing into a ball.

It was a short reprieve, for the *contented* devil was eager for more flesh.

She shook like a leaf as he cooed and fussed, kissing healing bruises, whispering words of love against her skin. "Come now, my Pearl. Let me show you my love."

It was almost impossible to speak. "This is not love."

Groaning out a blissfully broken laugh, the man licked her tears. "In my thousands of years ruling our kind, I have never cared for a single female with such devoted attention. Not one of my own flock have I used since you became my possession—no matter how the slavering bitches beg for it. I have filled your home with treasures; drained many humans night after night so my face might please you and my blood might be sweet." A lingering kiss was pressed to her slack mouth. "My entire existence is faithful to my delicate daywalker and the light she shares with me."

Too much had been done in the short hours since she'd woken in the cursed room. Clinging to a pillow as if it could offer salvation, she buried her face and cried, "You promised to be gentle."

"Is this not bliss?" Tangling his fingers through her hair, he forced her head back, drew her body to his chest, and sighed. "When you weep for me, I can taste the sunshine in your tears. When I drain you almost to the point of death, I can even stand in it for a few short minutes before I begin to burn. Whoever raped your mother and left her alive after the feed has my gratitude."

That wasn't love, his words were not soothing, and Pearl was in misery. "I don't have a mother."

"I know." Amused, he nipped at her ear. "The fact you were even conceived, given the odds, is miraculous… almost impossible. She would have died in labor as you fought your way out."

"What?"

"I know all your secrets, Pearl. I know about the Jesuit priest at the Mission Orphanage in California. I know how he hung you by the neck from a tree for three days when you were a little girl because he found you drinking the blood of rats. I know about the exorcisms, the beatings, the rapes. You have told me everything about you. Despite your misgiving at this moment, you adore me. I'm your savior. No soul can hurt you but me, and I always put you back together."

He was insane, absolutely crazy, and she felt the evil in him with every breath they shared. "You said you wouldn't hurt me if I was obedient."

"You enjoy pain, Pearl. You crave the things only I can do to you. How can you fully embrace pleasure otherwise?"

He had just ripped out her insides and swallowed them while she'd screamed for mercy. God might not be real, as he'd never once answered her prayers, but Pearl grasped that the devil existed. He'd found her as the priests said he would, and now he was going to eat up her soul. "I don't want you to hurt me."

"No?" A smile made his voice playful. "What is it that you think you want?"

Sobbing she said, "God's forgiveness."

"For what, being born? There is no creature more evil than this false God you think to worship over me."

She knew her prayers and her sins. "I want to go to heaven."

"I was turned before your Christian God came

into being. This religion, like all others, was created by humans so they might rule over other humans. Your Jesus never existed. There was no virgin birth or cantering angels in the skies of Bethlehem. Every last drop of it is a lie." Turning her body into the crook of his, he promised, "What is real is what is before you. Now, tell me you love me before I grow jealous."

He was talking her in circles, and Pearl felt he'd done so thousands of times. Her own tongue could not break from the cycle. "I was obedient and still you hurt me. If I tell you I love you, you will hurt me again."

"True." The monster seemed appeased, even gratified by her statement. "My Pearl, isn't honesty a beautiful thing?"

Before she could answer, Darius had her splayed on her belly with supernatural speed. Face pressed to the blankets, she bit back a scream, the feel of something boiling hot penetrating the cavity he'd torn apart. True, the damage had healed, but unlike the first time he'd taken her that night, she was ill prepared for such brutality.

Clawing at the bed, trying to find purchase, she pitched deeper into the mattress with his every thrust.

Struggles and pained grunts only drove him on. He wanted her to fight back.

He wanted to steal.

Going limp did not save her either.

A muscular forearm flexed around her throat, a fist once again knotted in her hair, and he bent her back until her spine screamed. Roaring like the devil he was, Darius slammed his cock into her body, snapping his hips violently against her backside.

He denied her air. Twisted as she was, there was nothing but him to hold on to. She couldn't even see his eyes, only red velvet bed curtains that blurred as her world tripped between conscious and unconscious. Pain and true suffering.

But in there, under all the malevolence was a twinge and a lesson.

She was only allowed to be limp if he made her limp. She was only allowed to scream if he made her scream.

Pearl was a possession. She was a *treasure*.

One he could control physically or mentally, the point driven home when the tendrils of his dominion invaded her thoughts and tempted her to revel in the violence.

The instant her cracked psyche gave in, flashing fangs tore through his wrist and the spurting wound was pressed to her slack mouth.

Absolution arrived. She swallowed.

As he fucked her, she drank.

Gurgling around a mouthful, Pearl felt herself

dragged to a higher state of being. High on his power, she could feel everything: each shredding thrust of a veined cock moving through skin not quite lubricated enough to facilitate smooth passage. She could feel the microscopic tears healing even as they split open anew. Overwrought nerves throbbed from both pleasure and pain, for he had found a place inside her body where, textured skin ached for punishment.

Under her knees, the bedsheets were slimy with blood, with bits of her that had escaped his feast, and with the very fluid he had accused her of spilling earlier.

She had indeed wet the bed, but it was not with piss.

Twisted by the glory of such perfect pain, what was dry became drenched. It ran down her thighs, clung like droplets of rain to the hair on his tight balls.

He abused her, left her aching and bone broken, and drew her greedy cunt through the worst sort of debasement and bliss.

Belly sloshing with his blood, she moved past fear straight into the red fires of the hell he'd designed for her. She came with such power it fractured her crumbling mind into pieces no amount of sweet words or broken promises would ever put back together.

You worship only me. He whispered the words into her mind. *I am your God.*

Darius slid from her twitching insides, cock hard as rock and pulsating as its master rolled his drooling conquest to her back. Thighs straddling her head, glorying in the smears of his blood over her chin, lips, and cheeks, he commanded, "Open your mouth. You are to swallow this too."

She didn't understand, and from his feral grin, it was obvious he took great pleasure in her innocence. Though could it be called innocence? Night after night did he not use his treasure, do unspeakable things to her, and work his evil over her body? After he was done, did he not strip away her thoughts and leave her a shell to wake again in this cold room, startled and scared.

A blank slate he could paint with blood.

A stupid girl he could pin down, where he might relish the pleasure of watching the shock on her face as he forced his cock past her lips and down her throat, choking her and denying her air.

Tongue pressed flat, her blunt teeth scraping the sides of his shaft, he ruthlessly fucked her mouth. When she began to bite, something changed, a look in the fiery red eyes, and Pearl swore that meat down her throat kicked.

The devil roared, pressing forward with such strength he tore out bits of her hair.

Salty tang burned like bile, coating her tongue, stinging her throat, and dripping from the corners of her swollen lips. Mashing his pelvis to her skull, Darius ushered more of that poison down his pulsating shaft and straight into her belly.

He held her that way after the last drop was spilled, watching her suffocate as if the view were magnificent.

Frantic for air, she begged with wide, wet eyes.

He smiled, yet did not move. "Speak of your God again, Pearl. Name him."

Scratching at his thigh, working her throat around his softening tool, she garbled, desperate to form the sounds of his name in a bid for freedom.

A satisfied cock popped from her lips, bloody vomit and tears following.

Much of what he had given her was spilled, cum and blood pooling on the bed. As she heaved, he patted her head, as if a good dog has performed well.

Arms came around her. Cuddled to her back despite the mess, he pressed his lips to her ear. "There is no reason to be afraid of the demands I make on your body. I would never truly harm you past the point your body might regenerate."

She was sobbing, coughing between gasps. "And tomorrow I will have forgotten, and you will do this again."

"Hush, child." Darius kissed the back of her head, sliding his fingers over her ribs, across a sick belly, and lower still, until he cupped her bruised sex. "You've pleased me. As a reward, I swear to be the sweet lover you wish for tomorrow. I'll fool you into smiles and laughter. When I fuck you, I won't draw blood. You have my word."

His word meant nothing to her. "And you have mine that I will hate you tomorrow as much as I hate you today."

He smiled, and let his finger penetrate where she was slippery with his cum. There they played no matter her sulking or lingering discomfort. "You love me, kara sevde, of that I have no doubt."

7

There were so many pages, unfamiliar entry after entry—all of them in *her* choppy handwriting. Yet, each lacked a date, filling up the tome that sat upon the room's solitary desk with a vague story of her time in this stone room.

I did not sleep last night, and when Darius came to me again, he smiled as if he knew I'd waited for his return. Bone tired, I was poor company, but he was kind to me. He even offered an explanation. My sentence in this room, he claimed, is twice the lifetime of the man I killed.

Chadwick Parker had not been a young man, and I worry I might be trapped here for near a century.

How many times had Pearl read this first entry?

It was impossible to know, but the page was growing worn and the book was filled with hundreds if not thousands of similarly pinned memories.

Darius held my hand when I grew sad at this news, claimed he hated to see my anguish. That is why he enforces his gift. My memory each night is wiped away so I might be spared from a monotonous eternity in prison. One day he'll hold my hand as I am set free. One day, I'll be allowed to meet others like me. I'll never be alone again.

Flipping through the journal, Pearl looked for something she couldn't pin. Over and over this Darius character was mentioned, but so far, she'd seen no sign of anyone in the cramped cell. Which was well and good. Yet something about the book was disturbing, obvious in its wrongness, but with no explanation.

Pages were missing, torn out. Gone forever.

Why?

Why remove pages from the journal? What had been written on them that Darius didn't want her to see?

Had she torn them out? And if she had, why do it?

Letting the book thump back on the desktop, Pearl looked over the grotesque grandness of the items piled inside her cell. From the red velvet draping the walls, to the jewels scattered over desk and crevice, everything seemed staged—like an altar.

Like an offering.

What would a girl locked in a room need with jewels? She was hardly even dressed in little more than lace bound by a sash around her middle.

She was also sporting dried blood under her nails and she smelled in need of a bath.

But there was no water, no urn, only a chamber pot of sorts that was uncomfortable to use.

There wasn't even a rat scurrying around for her to catch and eat.

Then again, according to the massive tome on the desk, she drank her meals from the mysterious Darius. In flowery language she even described the taste and how addicting it might be.

Pearl didn't use flowery language. A great many of the entries she scanned didn't sound like her at all.

Had he told her what to write?

More importantly, if she had been the one to tear out a page, where would she have hidden notes in this crypt?

Running her hands under the heavy mattress had led to nothing. Nooks in the wall were explored, the space behind paintings, even the trunk of scandalous clothing at the foot of the bed.

There was nothing but dust.

Dust?

Stamping her foot, Pearl felt the earth under the room's sumptuous rug. Things could be buried in dirt.

Like bodies.

Or trapped women.

Throwing back a corner of the rug, brushing aside dried rushes, damp earth met her fingers. Clawing at it here and there did naught but pit the ground. Fueled by a growing need for answers, Pearl threw handfuls of earth aside, careless of where they fell.

"You won't find what you're looking for there."

Crouched like a spider and panting as if she'd just run a race, Pearl cut a glance over her shoulder and hissed.

The mystery man himself stood like a beautiful beacon. And he was smiling at her, serene and unthreatening.

"Darius?"

A winged eyebrow arched. "Yes, Pearl?"

He obviously knew what she was up to, and seemed unconcerned. Tickled even. "Where are the missing pages?"

Walking toward a fantastical painting of an ancient warlord, the stranger pulled back a bit of torn canvas to display a nook. "Sometimes I find them here." He then changed course, moving to a stone in the wall that came away easily when jiggled. "And often here."

Both cavities were empty. Whatever she'd hidden away had been lost. And he had known to look for them. Nervous despite his kind expression, Pearl asked, "Why do you take them away?"

The handsome man's smile grew charmed. "Take them? I *collect* and keep them for you." He pointed to a small, obvious box on the desk. A place Pearl had ignored in her hunt.

Wiping dirtied hands on the impractical lace gown, Pearl crept forward, untrusting and cautious. It was as he claimed. Inside the jeweled box, the folded notes were haphazardly stacked.

Once she stood before them, he crossed the room. Appearing out of thin air behind her body.

His heat met her back. Lips to her ear, breath warm, he asked, "Do you want to play a game?"

Her fingers hovered over the notes. Buzzing nervously from the intimate way he brushed against her, Pearl whispered, "What kind of game?"

"For every note you choose to read, I earn a kiss from my beloved treasure."

It was a trick. Men were never forthcoming. But there was something deeper than cautious intuition that warned she needed to see what was on those stolen pages. "One kiss for one note?"

A rich smile in his voice, the man nuzzled closer. "A kiss, my love, nothing more."

Delving in, a random scrap of paper was chosen, pulled free, and unfolded.

Darius is the devil and you are in hell.

A hearty chuckle shook her body, the man pressed to her back extremely amused. "I do so love the look on your face when you read that one. In those first precious moments, you don't want to believe it. You'll turn and look me over from head to toe. Where are the horns? Where is the tail and cloven hooves? What reason might you have to think I am this character from your nightmares? Maybe it was written as a joke. Maybe, we'd argued that day... Perhaps you'd fallen gravid and grown *difficult*."

Fear crawled up her spine and blood ran cold no matter how warm the body at her back. Turning her head so she might glimpse the one wrapping his arms around her torso, Pearl met his glowing red eyes.

His gaze burned all the brighter, fangs slowly descending behind a positively elated smile. Teasing in the meanest voice she'd ever heard, Darius hummed, "Or, maybe it's absolutely true."

Mortally afraid, she stood there, a hairsbreadth from those teeth, and asked, "What does gravid mean?"

He brought a hand to her cheek, reminding her that there was a price. A kiss for a note. After all, there were rules to this *game*. Fingers pinched her chin, turning her attention back to the box. "I never claimed questions were a part of our fun."

One folded page would not be enough. Snatching up another, she tore it in her haste to read what was waiting.

He raped me over and over until I bled from every hole a man might abuse on a woman. I begged him to stop, and he laughed.

"That's two kisses now, my Pearl."

Fat, silent drops slipped over trembling cheeks. She reached for a third.

He's never going to let you out. Find a way to kill yourself.

A tongue traced the shell of her ear, followed by a low rumble. "But how would you do it? All your wounds heal almost instantly thanks to the strength my blood has given you."

Shivering, Pearl wrapped her arms around her middle, the heat emanating from the man pressed to her back worthless. "I don't want to read anymore."

"Three kisses are owed me then, sweet treasure." With a flourish, he spun her about, the desk cutting off any chance of retreat. Sniffing at her hair, he demanded like a spoiled prince. "I'll claim the first one now."

After only a few moments in his presence, the idea was repugnant no matter how handsome the stranger might be.

"We had a deal, Pearl. Honor it, and see how reasonable I can be. Why be so frightened of words on a page?"

Because unlike the book, those hidden words seemed real. Very real, as if a locked corner of her mind was pounding against a wall, trying to warn her danger was here.

Play his game or resist, what would lead to a more favorable outcome when trapped with the devil?

Standing on tiptoe, Pearl pressed a chaste kiss to sculpted, smirking lips.

It would seem chastity was of no interest to Darius. His tongue slipped into her mouth, delving to undulate inside. Razor sharp teeth nipped, drew blood that he sucked into his mouth with a satisfied groan.

Lips were abandoned for her jaw, his mouth working its way next to her neck.

It was there he sank in those fangs.

The pain was extraordinary.

Legs giving out, it was only the strength of the man that kept her upright as he drained a punctured vein.

He feasted no matter how she fought, until her

vision narrowed to a pinpoint. Limp, useless, she hung like a ragdoll.

Pain seemed to fade, her body ready to release the spirit where it could leave this room and go to God.

The sweet silence of death so close, she craved it. Smiled at the coming light.

Until Darius dropped her.

Weak, twisted like a discarded marionette, she could only groan while the man licked his lips and grinned.

He wasn't going to let her go to the light. No, he wanted to keep her in his darkness forever. Isn't that what the missing page claimed?

Trying to get to her knees, to crawl under the desk as if it might offer shelter, earned a barked laugh.

"Kara sevde, there will be none of that." He seized her ankle, and pulled her under his crouching body. "What would you gain by hiding that pretty face from me?"

"Help me." Her plea was not for him; it was said out of sick desperation that God might listen.

"Hush, child. You are not going to die." A rumble of demonic glee, of a thirst for more than blood, moved from sculpted lips to an unwilling ear. "But I will grant you sleep. Enjoy my mercy. But when you wake, two more kisses are owed."

8

F loating in warmth, Pearl was certain this had to be what heaven might offer—weightlessness, intoxication by a sense of perfection.

Nothing could touch her here.

Nothing, until softness brushed her brow, urging lashes to part to the glow of gold.

Candles burned, flickering soft light off a cracked oil painting. It was the image of a woman tending to goats on a rolling hillside, beautiful by any stretch. The sun shone as if real, more real than the dots of light blurring in the periphery of her vision.

"That, my dear, is our favorite painting. Can you not feel the wind in the bent grass as you look upon it? Seeing it now, I almost remember the scent of a field warmed by summer."

Shifting, only just growing aware of her body, led water to slosh and splash against her skin. Blurry vision settled on a man so near her face, she could smell the soap on his skin. Following the line of his arm from neck to hands, she found his sleeves were rolled up, his forearms dripping wet and half submerged.

Pearl felt weightless and warm because she was prone, naked, in a copper tub… a stranger hovering over her.

A strong hand came to her jaw, angling her lolling head back to rest on the waiting towel. "It's only I, your Darius."

Certain she was drunk, Pearl sucked her bottom lip. It was smeared with flavor. Wine? Or was that bourbon? Reaching up to gather what dripped from the corner of her mouth, she looked to her fingers and found blood.

A deep, perfect red.

Her throat ached to lick it up, craving that crimson bead as she'd never wanted anything before. "I don't…"

The man winked. "Know how you got here? We were playing a game, and I'm afraid you grew utterly drained."

Entranced with that red dot, Pearl brought it back to her lips so it would not be wasted.

The man had other ideas.

Catching her wrist, he brought the finger to his lips and sucked it clean.

When she tried to snatch her finger from the heat of his mouth, he pricked her flesh, laughing when she squealed. Then he gave her a dazzling smile.

Two long fangs, milky white, glimmered in the low light. "There is nothing to fear. Look at your finger, Pearl. It is already mending."

Mouth agape, she was unsure exactly which topic was most in need of immediate attention: the fact she was naked, obviously being bathed by a striking stranger. The fact there was another person like her. One who spoke warmly to her, knew her name, and seemed *almost familiar*. Or, the fact that her finger was healing right before her eyes.

Nudity was addressed first, both arms slipping so they might cover where her breasts bobbed in steaming water.

This earned a breathy chuckle. "Your shyness strikes me as particularly charming in this moment."

Knowing her cheeks were a vivid pink, Pearl tried his name. "You said your name was Darius. I don't… I don't know you. I don't know how I got here. Is this the hospital? Have I been ill?"

Red eyes, that's what they were—red as blood and glowing like an ember ready to set the world to flame. "Darius, yes, and I am at your service, my Pearl. And, yes, you do know me. You know your lover very well, you just don't remember me. You see, we meet anew each night in your chamber."

She had to be drugged or ill. Not a word he said made sense.

Neither the painting nor the handsome man held her attention. It was the walls she looked to, the chipped hunks of stone, the lack of windows. She was in a cell, blocked in a corner by a screen that hid the remainder of the room. "Why wouldn't I remember you?"

Her chin was caught, Pearl made to meet the eye of the stranger. "So that you might be happy, always. Time has a way of twisting our kind. You have the gift of constant newness. Your God has blessed you. He dotes on you."

"My God?"

"Every day is fresh. Every time I touch you, it's the first time. Every time I kiss you, you still blush. I am the perpetual bridegroom, and you are my darling treasure. There is much joy to be had in this."

Men did not speak that way to women; they didn't look upon them as if they were going to swallow them whole. She sunk lower in the water as if it might shield her from the weight of his gaze.

Darius tutted. "You wish for privacy so you might dry yourself and dress. That is unnecessary. I know your body inside and out. There is no cause to flinch or try to hide in the tub." He picked up her hand and began to clean dirt from under her nails, no matter how she fought to pull it back. "*I* shall finish bathing you, *I* will dry you, *I* will dress you. Then, *I* will feed you."

He made her sound like some doll, tutting and clucking when he found a broken nail or a hanging bit of cuticle. "Such a mess. Be still."

Be still. The command rang inside her skull, and still she became. She couldn't move, not even to blink or turn her eyes from his scowl.

Next he soaped her shoulder, the remaining length of her arm, Pearl stiff and unable to respond.

Strangers didn't touch this way. They didn't issue unspoken commands that a body was physically incapable of ignoring.

"You may breathe and speak, Pearl."

Throat dry, Pearl sucked in air. "How did you…"

An impish wink, and he kissed the tips of her clean fingers. "I'm your God, remember?"

"And you said… lover." She had never had a

lover. Men had never touched her for her benefit. They certainly had never buffed her nails. "Have we... umm?"

A subtle twitch came to the corner of the man's mouth. "Have we umm what?"

He was going to make her say it, Pearl blushing all the harder. "Known one another well?"

Moving slow enough to assure he had her total attention, the man dipped his fingers under the bubbling soap scum. His wrist followed, his forearm. "I have known you in every possible way."

Fingers crept between her thighs, separating folds, to tease a place that made her gasp when treated to small circles of friction.

His head hovered lower, Darius observing her parted lips and dazed eyes. "You suffer such attention beautifully, and I think you always will. I dare you to tell me you do not enjoy this."

A noise caught in her throat as he breached her, a single finger wriggling inside that place men liked to damage and use.

Only his attention brought no pain. There were gasps of surprise instead, little sounds coming from lips that spoke of trepidation, confusion, and a drugged hunger for more.

Water began to splash when his exploration grew more vigorous—what had been slow and meticulous became wild and unbearable. Head back against the lip of the tub, Pearl squeezed her eyes shut and found a rush unlike anything she'd known. Before she might stop herself, she cried out and lurched, spilling water and soaking the man's shirt front.

He pressed a kiss to her slack lips as if she were some sleeping beauty waiting for the prince to wake her. "That is only a taste of what we have shared."

In her wide, dazed eyes sat sluggish relief. This was no monster...

Hovering over her mouth, he smiled again. "Kiss me, my Pearl. Kiss me, and I shall be sweet."

Kissing was not a familiar activity any more than the odd sensations of having a man touch her gently between her legs. All the others had shunted in ugly, hard flesh for their own pleasure. Usually they drew blood.

Certain now that she was drunk, ill, completely mad, she gave in and pressed her lips to his— because all of this had to be a dream, and rare sweet dreams should be savored.

There was an instant reward. His fingers went back to teasing that magical place even as his tongue tangled and teased hers. Moaning under him, unsure why her body moved as it did, Pearl gripped the edges of the tub as if that might anchor her in this wonderful sensation.

As she was about to crest, shatter, and be reborn, he stopped. Pulling his fingers from the fluttering hungry part of her body, his lips followed suit. A string of spittle stretching between them before it snapped. "Stand. I want to look at you all clean and shining in candlelight."

She leveraged her weight against the tub, completely graceless as she fought feeble legs to stand. Without the comfort of the water, she felt like death warmed over.

"Ungh." Unsteady, she swayed, and muttered, "I have been ill."

Seated on his stool, he began to touch the tottering woman, humming approval when she leaned into his hands for support. "Fragile little kitten, you're hungry." He crooked his fingers, commanding her from the tub and to his lap. "Come."

Ravenous, in fact. Swallowing, she looked to the thigh he indicated should serve as her seat, and muttered a dazed, "I'm wet. I'll leave a mark."

"Yes, you are. Now obey me. Come." Flat out chuckling, he gave her hand a yank. She tripped from the tub, caught in his arms, and draped over his knee.

Breathless, she gawked over her shoulder when he set his hand to her rump and explored. As he leered and toyed between her cheeks, she felt more and more the prostitute and less the lover.

Exposed, weak, and growing cold, she sucked her lower lip between her teeth and tried to push away.

"No wriggling!"

She heard the sound of the smack before it registered how hard he'd struck her.

The flesh of her ass jiggled, stung horribly, and would bruise. But it was her pride that was far more damaged. Red faced, mortified and aching, she shook her head but had no words.

"Had you sat as you'd been told, I would have cuddled you dry with sweet kisses and soft words." Drawing up a soft towel from where it rested beside the bath, he began to blot droplets away from her bowed back. He palmed her ass, squeezed that bruised flesh, and grinned when she looked away in shame. "I'm only teasing, Pearl. Who could resist such a view?"

Gently he turned her, sat the shamefaced woman on his knee and pressed a tender kiss to her temple. "We were playing a game before you fell asleep. I think we should play another."

Aching, aroused, unwell, and starving, she sighed. "I'm not very good at games."

Nuzzling her wet hair, he whispered, "But you win so often."

"I'm cold."

"You owe me one more kiss." He was already at her mouth, sucking the trapped lip from her teeth before he added, "One more kiss, then we play a new game."

The pressure, the friction, even the sharp edges of his teeth, all of it was his doing. She was trapped under the onslaught, gasping for air and shocked to feel the stirrings return between her thighs. But as it was, she could not kiss him, not with his tongue already in her mouth. If that was his game, she had no way to win. All she could do was try to make words that were swallowed, ignored, and grunted at.

But she was growing warm again. Every last attention he lavished on her felt... nice.

A rush grew in the place he'd explored under the water, a plumpness Pearl did not recognize that made her want to press harder to his thigh, and forget the lingering soreness of her ass.

When he gave her a moment of breath, she panted, found herself squirming, and just about fainted when he suddenly took her nipple between his teeth. "Is this the game?"

Grunting a non-answer, those long teeth he'd used to cut her thumb were planted into her breast. Sucking her nipple, tonguing it, a mix of searing pain and unknown pleasure mingled as he drank the scant blood that ran.

Pulling his mouth from her breast, teeth red with her blood, those eyes burned with hellfire. "Bite me."

Gawking at the small trickle of blood that ran from her skin, staring at the man who'd left the mark of his mouth on her, Pearl felt her gums tingle. When she tongued each tip, she found two teeth descended, far too short to even break skin.

Reaching up to touch the useless tips with her finger, shocked she hadn't noticed earlier, she balked. "They're gone."

The fervent stranger didn't care. He took her hair and drew her mouth to his neck.

The smell she found there set her to salivating. The needle-like pain on her scalp from his overly enthusiastic grip forgotten as her tongue traced a pulsating vein.

The man moaned in a way Pearl had only ever heard when men were finished with her.

For once, she liked it.

She bit and gnawed, did everything she could to get that vein to burst open and spray her mouth with what was hidden inside.

Nothing worked.

Well, something was working. The man's hand had delved into his trousers and between their tangled bodies he was pumping his fist.

Unfed hunger led to sharp frustration. Her teeth

were too short to pierce, her jaw too weak to break salty skin. Everything she needed was right there, so close but unattainable.

But then the smell of blood filled her nose.

His warm, perfect blood.

Yet it was not coming from his neck.

She slunk to the floor without thought, hand around an organ that dripped rubies from an even more generously throbbing vein. When she tried to suck just from the side of that thing, strong hands repositioned her skull. It was put between her teeth, forced toward her throat until she gagged and had trouble swallowing the pooling blood.

All she wanted was a rich drink, annoyed with the man bobbing her head up and down.

Swallowing with that thick organ down her throat became necessary. Breath was forgotten, all that mattered was the struggle against what held her down and wasted blood she *needed* in her belly. Just as the vein closed and her meal was cut short, something salty sprayed against her tongue.

Made to swallow it in her quest for the final drops of perfection, Pearl retched.

Flailing, half drowning and unable to breathe, she felt the weight on her skull give in. Falling back in a graceless pile, sucking in air as if she'd been under water, Pearl saw the man, his trousers gaping, his mouth open and head thrown back.

It was then she realized just what she'd so ravenously drunk from.

His cock.

That part of a man they liked to stick like a brand into a woman—the thing that burned and brought pain.

That had been his game.

Something was running from the corner of her lips, a wasted drop both salty and sweet.

Darius caught it with his thumb, pushed it back between her shocked lips before using the tip of his finger to close her gaping mouth. "Did you enjoy your dinner?"

There was no answer. The blood had been overly delicious, the things he'd been doing during her feast unrecognized. It couldn't be normal, a woman's mouth on a man's body that way. Embarrassed, unsure if she could bring herself to stop cringing on the floor, Pearl muttered, "Why would you do that?"

Stroking her cheek, Darius smiled. "Swallow my cum like a good girl. Taste it on your velvet tongue. Next I'll leave it dripping from your tight cunt. After that, there is another place on your body I like to bury my seed. Play nicely, and I'll fill your belly with another mouthful of what makes you swoon before I fuck your ass."

Pearl looked back at the thing she'd just had

down her throat, not at all eager for it to be back inside any part of her body. Just as she was no longer eager to pretend this was a pleasant dream.

He was still hard.

Usually, after they had pushed in, thrust about, and told her to stop screaming, those things got smaller.

Taking the meat of his cock in hand, the man crooned, "You still owe me a kiss. Press your lips here, and thank me for all I gave you."

She didn't want it in her throat again; all she had wanted to taste was the blood.

This dream was no longer enticing. In fact, now that she'd had a meal, it didn't feel dream-like at all.

It was real.

Darius was real.

She was in a room with a man who had put his organ in her mouth.

An organ she had licked manically for drops of blood that did not make her retch as human blood did...

Semen did not taste appealing, the belief confirmed a moment later when he fisted her hair, and led her mouth to the tip where a drop of tang remained.

She kissed it as she was told to, felt her stomach rumble and her throat itch.

Mostly, she felt unclean.

"Are you thinking of the mean old priest?"

A flood of terrible memories intruded as if a dam had broken behind her eyes. This interlude had not been the first time she'd done this. How could she have forgotten something so horrible?

A cry caught in her throat, one that turned to a whimper of degradation.

A hand came to her bowed head and stroked her hair. "And that, kara sevde, is why I do not allow you to remember. That is why every night for you starts new and clean."

Who would want to have such dark things always lurking in their mind? The stranger had given her blood that had not made her sick, he had given her pleasure in the tub, and then he had given her the memory of a terrible past. Falling to his feet, she put her lips to his shoes and begged he take the nightmares away again.

Voice like iron, Darius warned his treasure, "I shall take all he did from your mind, but remember this fractured moment tonight should you question your life in my care, buck my requests, or shy from my attention. There is no suffering in this room but the torment you bring upon yourself. I would give you the bliss of permanent innocence. I would fill you with pleasure. Thank me for it."

Sobbing, she vigorously held to his leg. "Thank you."

And then the rancid memories that had broken her heart were gone. Confused why she was even upset, the tears stopped.

Cupping her face, he wiped wet trails from her cheeks. "Your life with me, in this place, can be sunshine or it can be darkness. Every night, the choice is yours."

9

Over several hours, Darius taught her the meaning of rapture.

And the price…

His attention had been so wondrous that she'd almost forgotten how degrading it was to be used. Yet no matter how he kissed and touched, under her joy she knew all he did was for his own entertainment. He wanted to see her beg like a whore, knew what nerves to manipulate to earn a slattern's response.

Twisted by the expertise of a practiced lecher, she'd cried out, unsure of the exact moment his body had pushed her past sanity. For only a mad woman would have thanked him for fucking her so raw she'd bled.

She'd even tangled her hands in his hair when

he'd pulled her cunt to his mouth so he might feast on their shared fluids.

When his cum and her blood were smeared over his chin, red eyes burned and his long teeth shone in the candlelight. "Turn over. Bow your head to the covers."

She'd obeyed without question.

"Tell me you love me." Glistening cockhead notched between her cleft, he'd raked his nails over her hips.

More of her blood spilled from the gashes, just as the foul words fell from a drunken tongue. "I love you."

"Call me your God!" He spread her cheeks, sluicing forward through all the mess that dripped from her cunt.

It felt as if there was a knock on the door of her skull, a mental caution to refuse such blasphemy. There was only one God. *The* God. The creator of the world who'd promised to deliver her from evil.

Evil shunted in, straight into a hole that was unslick, upstretched, and unprepared. Bawling, flailing while tears fell, she screamed, "You are my God!"

The creature tearing her ass apart roared. It was not the sound of a man in pleasure, but a demon set free from the abyss. Unwilling to turn her head, she imagined great wings had spread behind her tormentor to beat the air as he pulled her down that blood-stained cock.

The damage was extensive, for the devil had been unshackled.

He claimed his due from her flesh.

A single, worthless soul.

One that God had rejected long ago. One that was treasured by a monster who relished perverting love into pain.

Empty of hope, full of cock.

That was how she died inside. Any proselyte knew there would be no forgiveness in the eyes of the Lord for this.

The flesh agreed, twisting up around the pulsating intrusion. Her cunt fluttered, opening up like a little mouth seeking a sweet kiss. The nub at the top of her sex throbbed as if an overripe berry near bursting.

Despite how he ravaged her hips, it was *her* touch that found that pulped flesh and dove in to fill the empty hole. He bellowed a sickening laugh to see little fingers play.

When she came, it was while riding a scream of pain.

He sprayed white globs of stinging grossness so far inside her, it would linger like a stain she could never push out.

What had she done?

On fire, pinned under the weight of a monster lazy with slaked lust, her tears fell hot and free.

At last that organ was shrinking, slowly worming its way out of her ass. But the mark he'd made on her, the blasphemy he'd drawn from foolish lips would never seep out, no matter how many holes she tore in her flesh.

"I am lost…"

Filth crusted nails raked her chin, forcing her to twist her neck at an impossible angle so that one large blue eye might find his devious smile. "I so ador—"

The floor dropped out from under them, and with an earsplitting crash, dust and debris snowed down upon her room. It was as if the earth itself shook, as if it worked its jaws, intent on devouring the vampire whore and the beast panting on her back.

"HE WOULDN'T DARE!" Darius pulled away, careless of the damage he caused, or the detritus that followed the path of his dick from her anus. Once on his feet, the ground wrenched again, almost upsetting the devil's balance. "You." Turning his fury on the bleeding woman soiling the coverlet. "Stay there! This insurrection will be crushed at once."

Through tears, Pearl saw the air bend, distort,

and Darius, the devil she'd named as her God, vanished.

It would be easy to say that the rocking of the earth which sent her candelabras toppling over was a sign of her salvation. It would be easy to claim divinity smiled upon her.

It didn't.

In fact, no one came to smile, threaten, bleed her, or denounce.

Hours she lay under a ceiling that dusted her room in a fog of ancient dirt. In that time her body mended.

Darius did not return.

One by one the candles began to flicker and wane. All the soft golden light of her cell faded, snuffed out to scent the air with a wisp of smoke. It was not until the last three had almost met their end before Pearl found the will to rise from the bed. New tapers were lit, and had she been wiser, she would have rationed her meager supply.

Rocking herself in the shadowy room, surrounding by fine paintings, by jewels, by sumptuous furnishing and a tub grown cold, she saw the cell for what it was.

A tomb.

Her tomb.

Day's passed, Pearl sleeping anywhere but the soiled bed.

Starving, down to her last candle, she read through the book she'd found on the desk, and knew the gnawing in her gut was more than hunger.

This was a bad place.

A bad place where she had been tempted, and spoken terrible words.

When she opened the filigreed box on the desk, when she found the notes, she didn't weep. After all, didn't the church teach that there was no such thing as victims of the devil? She had come to him of her own accord.

She had killed Chadwick Parker. She had served as the demon's slut.

She had renounced her God under the ecstasies only the prince of darkness might offer.

And every word on those torn notes was true.

She was in Hell.

Damned, Pearl snuffed out the last candle before it might burn away. Pitch black filled her vision. Shuffling through the furniture, she found the stinking bed, and pulled the covers crusted in all things unholy over her body. There she lay, forgotten, abandoned, and without hope.

Just as she deserved.

Starvation drained her flesh over weeks. Shriveled, desiccated, she lay like an age worn corpse unable to blink. Yet, where the body failed the mind *persevered*.

She couldn't scream into that endless night. Eventually, even her chest no longer rose to draw breath. But awareness and desolation never faded.

Hell was a dedicated custodian. It refused to release her stolen soul.

Years, decades, passed trapped on that bed staring up into unyielding dark.

Alone.

Forgotten.

Forsaken.

Another corpse in the catacombs.

Thank you for reading CATACOMBS! Ready for more? The following dark romance, CATHEDRAL awaits. Do you long to #FreePearl? Her happily ever after awaits in THE RELIC.

Now, please enjoy an extended excerpt of CATHEDRAL...

CATHEDRAL
Cradle of Darkness, Book One

Edging closer, close enough that my stomach rumbled at his scent, the inevitable chastising began. "Jade, you wouldn't be so physically weak if you'd feed as you should. More importantly, starvation clouds your judgment. It makes you unreasonable."

"Malcom." I parroted his demeaning tone. "Despite my submission to having cameras all over my home, I do not enjoy having an audience while I'm being fucked." Angry, hating that this man had stood witness to another session of my degradation, I snapped. "You could have at least turned around!"

Faster than I by far, exponentially stronger, one moment Malcom was a comfortable distance away, the next his fingers carded through my fallen hair. "You need to feed."

How I hated that I jumped.

Against the undead, I was a piss-poor fighter. That didn't stop me from instantly shoving him so hard the wall he flew into cracked from the force.

"Don't touch me!"

He'd rebounded to his feet in a blur, completely unharmed by my outburst. Brushing dust from tailored black slacks, he had the audacity to smirk. "Pathetic, really. You can do better."

And then his fingers were playing with my hair again.

I couldn't effectively retaliate, because he was right. I was starving, and weakened, and so fucking tempted to tear into his flesh, that behind my lips, my fangs punched downward.

Embarrassing.

So I turned my head away instead, eyes locking on the dumpster as if failing to acknowledge him would make him disappear.

Lips at my ear, a willing throat far too close to my salivating mouth, Malcom murmured, "Give me your word that you'll feed tonight, and I'll leave you in peace."

Grinding my teeth, refusing to concede to such a blatant taunt, I hissed, "I'll eat."

Oh, I'd eat. I'd eat and I'd disgust the bane of my existence in a single swoop.

With the pitter patter of rats already creaking under the dumpster, as soon as one might skitter by, I'd snap it up and tear in.

Right there where he could see.

I'd suck that vermin dry and then grab another. Who cared that feeding from animals was forbidden, lowly? Agitated as I was, I didn't even care that I would most certainly be punished once my father found a hint of my action staining my memory.

He backed away at my agreement.

Once my eyes darted to where skittering was the loudest, Malcom knew what I was about. Silvery golden hair wafting about his shoulders like he was some goddamn phantom, he barked, "Jade, don't."

But I had already reached out. Fur filled my palm, and almost my mouth, before I realized that I held no rat.

A mewling kitten, dropped before I might scream.

Blood drained from my face. Vampire pale, I stared in horror as the feline scampered back to its hiding place, and I felt a thing I was forbidden from feeling.

"Look at me, Jade." Why did he dare sound so sympathetic? "The cat's gone. Look at me."

Gowned in Chanel couture, prettied, and coiffed, with cum running down my thigh, I didn't even attempt to pretend that we both didn't know why I trembled.

"It's gone. It's okay."

Before his fingertips might ghost over my shoulder, before I might have embarrassed myself further, I snapped. "I told you not to touch me!"

Hand hovering, still as the corpse he was,

Malcom obeyed. He even took two steps back. Only then did I make my eyes track from that sliver of dark under the dumpster to look at his face.

Like a carved marble statue, beautiful in the same unearthly way all undead were beautiful. It was like staring at God's favorite angel. Outranking almost every last withered soul in the hive, he'd never fallen into the habit of outlandish costumes.

Slacks, a fitted sweater. Utilitarian yet impeccably tailored.

And pity.

He was wearing pity on his impossibly attractive face. "It's ten minutes to midnight. I'll count this last mating towards your debt for tomorrow."

I would not let my wet eyes spill. "Fuck off, Malcom. If you think I'm falling for that, you're going to be disappointed."

His face returned to its normal state of smugness. "You're due home at sundown."

Wiping my nose on the back of my hand, I sighed at the ruin this evening had made of my dress. "And you're reminding me of a standing appointment why?"

"It is my duty to inform you when you have been summoned."

The exact thing he'd announced when he'd intruded on the Viking's interlude. "I see."

He'd interrupted on purpose. Technically he had not broken any rules. I hated when he did that.

Eyes like starlight, jaw flexing, Malcom dared another modicum of emotion. "Do you recall the exact reason why you dislike me, because I can't?"

I had no intention of playing this game with him.

But he muttered on, running a hand through his hair. "I remember *that day*. Why you grew upset when you saw a cat. I remember that you were wearing a blue dress with a red bow."

If his reason for existence was to torment me, he was doing a phenomenal job. "Funny that you remember that dress but don't remember why you sicken me."

"Funny that we remember anything..." The anger on his face washed away into deep consideration. Crossing his arms over his chest, my custodian sighed. "You haven't even reached a century in age, Jade. You're still such a blind, inexperienced child. Acting out without thinking. Refusing to eat. Pouting."

The light in his eyes, it was as if he thought I were cute. There was no reason I had to stand there and bear it. Brushing past, I made to exit the alley.

"I'll throw you a portal, Jade."

The very thought of taking Malcom's magical charity made me want to scream. "I'll walk. Thanks."

Despite my rejection, he cast a gate at the mouth of the alley, leaving me no other option. "If you'd have eaten, you'd have been able to summon your own."

Fucking prick.

Read **CATHEDRAL** now!

BORN TO BE BOUND
Alpha's Claim, Book One

She watched him bolt the door with a rod so thick it dwarfed her ankle, trapping her, cornering the Omega for mating. Unsure if Shepherd had heard, she used her feet to scoot away from the male until her back hit the wall, and tried again. "Food... we can't go out... hunted, forced. They're killing us." Her blown pupils looked up at the intimidating male and pleaded for him to understand. "You are *the* Alpha in Thólos, you hold control... we have no one else to ask."

"So you foolishly walked into a room full of feral males to ask for food?" He was mocking her, his eyes mean, even as he grinned.

The horror of the day, the sexual frustration of her heat, made Claire belligerently raise her head and meet his eyes. "If we don't get food, I'm dead anyway."

Seeing the female grimace through another cramping wave, Shepherd growled, an instinctual reaction to a breeding Omega. The noise shot right between her legs, full of the promise of everything she needed. His second, louder grumbled noise sang inside her, and a wave of warm slick drenched the floor below her swollen sex, saturating the air to entice him.

She could not take it. "Please don't make that noise."

"You are fighting your cycle," he grunted low and abrasive, beginning to pace, watching her all the while.

Shaking her head back and forth, Claire began to murmur, "I've lived a life of celibacy."

Celibacy? That was unheard of... a rumored story. Omegas could not fight the urge to mate. That was why the Alphas fought for them and forced a pair-bond to keep them for themselves. The smell alone drove any Alpha into a rut.

He growled again and the muscles of her sex clenched so hard she whined and curled up on the floor.

It was hard enough to make it through estrous locked in a room alone until the cycle broke, but his damn noise and the smell invading past the rotting stickiness of her clothing was breaking her insides apart.

The degrading way he spoke made her open her eyes to see the beast standing still, his massive erection apparent despite layers of clothing. "How long does your heat typically last, Omega?"

Shivering, suddenly loving the sound of that

lyrical rasp, she clenched her fists at her sides instead of beckoning him nearer. "Four days, sometimes a week."

"And you have been through them all in seclusion instead of submitting to an Alpha to break them?"

"Yes."

He was making her angry, furious even, with his stupid questions. Every part of her was screaming out that he should be stroking her and easing the need. *That it was his job*! With her hand still pressed over her nose and mouth, her muffled, broken explanation came as a jumbled, angry rant, Claire hissing, "I choose."

He just laughed, a cruel, coarse sound.

Omegas had become exceptionally rare since the plagues and the following Reformation Wars a century prior. That made them a valuable commodity which Alphas in power took as if it was their due. And in a city brimming with aggressive Alphas like Thólos, she'd been trapped in a life of feigning existence as a Beta just to live unmolested, spent a small fortune on heat-suppressants, and locked herself away with the other few celibates she knew when estrous came. Hidden in plain sight before Shepherd's army sprung out of the Undercroft and the government was slaughtered, their corpses left strung up from the Citadel like trophies.

Claire had been forced into hiding the very next day, when the unrest inspired the lower echelons of population to challenge for dominance. Where there had been order, suddenly all Thólos knew was anarchy. Those awful men just took any Omega they could find; killing mates and children in order to keep the women—to breed them or fuck until they died.

"What is your name?"

She opened her eyes, elated he was listening. "Claire."

"How many of you are there, little one?"

Trying to focus on a spot on the wall instead of the large male and where his beautiful engorged dick was challenging the zipper of his trousers, she turned her head to where her body craved to nest, staring with hunger at the collection of colorful blankets, pillows—a bed where everything must be saturated by his scent.

An extended growl warned, "You are losing your impressive focus, little one. How many?"

Her voice broke. "Less than a hundred... We lose more every day."

"You have not eaten. You're hungry." It was not a question, but spoken with such a low vibration that his hunger for *her* was apparent.

"Yesss." It was almost a whine. She was so near to pleading, and it wasn't going to be for food.

The prolonged answering growl of the beast compelled a gush of slick to wet her so badly, she was left sitting in a slippery puddle. Doubling over, frustrated and needy, she sobbed, "Please don't make that noise," and immediately the growl changed pitch. Shepherd began to purr for her.

There was something so infinitely soothing in that low rumble that she sighed audibly and did not bolt at his slow, measured approach. She watched him with such attention, her huge, dilated pupils a clear mark that she was so very close to falling completely into estrous.

Even when Shepherd crouched down low, he towered over her, all bulging muscle and musky sweat. She tried to say the words, "*Only instincts...*" but jumbled them so badly their meaning was lost.

Starting with the scarf, he unwound the items that tainted her beautiful pheromones, purring and stroking every time she whimpered or shifted nervously. When he pulled her forward to take away the reeking cloak, her eyes drew level with his confined erection. Claire's uncovered nose sniffed automatically at the place where his trousers bulged. In that moment all she wanted, all that she had ever wanted, was to be fucked, knotted, and bred by that male.

Only instincts...

Shepherd pressed his face to her neck and

sucked in a long breath, groaning as his cock jumped and began to leak to please her. He had gone into the rut, there was no changing that fact, and with it came a powerful need to see the female filled with seed, to soothe what was driving her to rub against her hand in such a frenzy.

The words were almost lost in her breath, "You need to lock me in a room for a few days..."

A feral grin spread. "You are locked in a room, little one, with the Alpha who killed ten men and two of his sworn Followers to bring you here." He stroked her hair, petting her because something inside told him his hands could calm her. "It's too late now. Your defiant celibacy is over. Either you submit willingly to me where I will rut you through your heat, or you may leave out that door where my men will, no doubt, mount you in the halls once they smell you."

Read BORN TO BE BOUND now!

ADDISON CAIN

USA TODAY bestselling author and Amazon Top 25 bestselling author, Addison Cain's dark romance and smoldering paranormal suspense will leave you breathless.
Obsessed antiheroes, heroines who stand fierce, heart-wrenching forbidden love, and a hint of violence in a kiss awaits.

For the most current list of exciting titles by Addison Cain, please visit her website: addisoncain.com

facebook.com/AddisonlCain
bookbub.com/authors/addison-cain
goodreads.com/AddisonCain

ALSO BY ADDISON CAIN

Don't miss these exciting titles by Addison Cain!

Standalone:

Swallow it Down

Strangeways

The Golden Line

The Alpha's Claim Series:

Born to be Bound

Born To Be Broken

Reborn

Stolen

Corrupted

Wren's Song Series:

Branded

Silenced

The Irdesi Empire Series:

Sigil

Sovereign

Que (coming soon)

Cradle of Darkness Series:

Catacombs

Cathedral

The Relic

A Trick of the Light Duet:

A Taste of Shine

A Shot in the Dark

Historical Romance:

Dark Side of the Sun

Horror:

The White Queen

Immaculate